Super Dad!

Roderick Hunt • Alex Brychta

OXFORD
UNIVERSITY PRESS

"Look at Dad," said Mum.

"Dad looks silly," said Wilma.

"No, he looks good," said
Wilf.

Dad put on a red nose.

"Oh!" said Wilma.
"Dad looks so silly."

Dad had a bucket.

"Put your money in here,"
he said.

Oh no! A man took Dad's money.

"Stop!" called Mum. "Come
back."

But the man didn't stop.

Dad got on a bike.

The man ran fast . . .

but Dad went faster.

"Got you," said Dad.

"Help!" said the man.

"Super Dad!" said Wilma.

Think about the story

Why did Wilma say that Dad looked silly?

What happened after the man took the bucket?

How did Dad stop the thief?

What would you like to dress up as?

A maze

Help Dad to catch the thief.